D0532240

DIAL BOOKS FOR YOUNG READERS

For Banana, who is a snake, and Abby Ranger, who is not.
And to Kate Harrison, thanks . . . a lot!
-T.S.

To Aimee and Steph
-M.L.

Dial Books for Young Readers
An imprint of Penguin Random House LLC, New York

Visit us online at penguinrandomhouse.com

Printed in China
ISBN 9780735230804

10 9 8 7 6 5 4 3 2 1

Hand lettering by Mike Lowery
Design by Jasmin Rubero
Text set in KG Blank Space

THIS IS KNOT.

THIS IS
NOT KNOT.

THIS IS
SNAKE.

HISSSS

KNOT ACHES TO BE LIKE SNAKE.

SNAKE CAN SLITHER.
KNOT CANNOT.
A LITTLE HELP?

SNAKE CAN
HISS.
YIKES
KNOT CANNOT.
BZZZ
OH NO, A GNAT!
HEY! GET OFF ME!

SNAKE CAN SWALLOW HER SUPPER WHOLE.

KNOT CANNOT.
(KNOT DOES NOT EAT SUPPER.)
I WISH I HAD A MOUTH.

SNAKE CAN EVEN SHED HER SKIN.
SNAKE LOOKS BRAND-NEW.

CAN KNOT LOOK
BRAND-NEW?
NO, HE'S
A FRAYED
KNOT.
HA
HA

CAN KNOT
DO THIS?

HOP. HOP.

KNOT CANNOT.

CAN KNOT DO THIS?

KNOT CANNOT.
KNOT BOBS.

CAN KNOT DO THIS?
KNOT CAN...
NOT.

WHAT CAN KNOT DO?

SNAKE TASTES THE AIR WITH HER TONGUE.

(NOT KNOT.)

OH NO!
DANGER!

BIRD
LANDS
NEARBY.

KNOT IS NOT AFRAID.

BIRD CANNOT SWALLOW KNOT

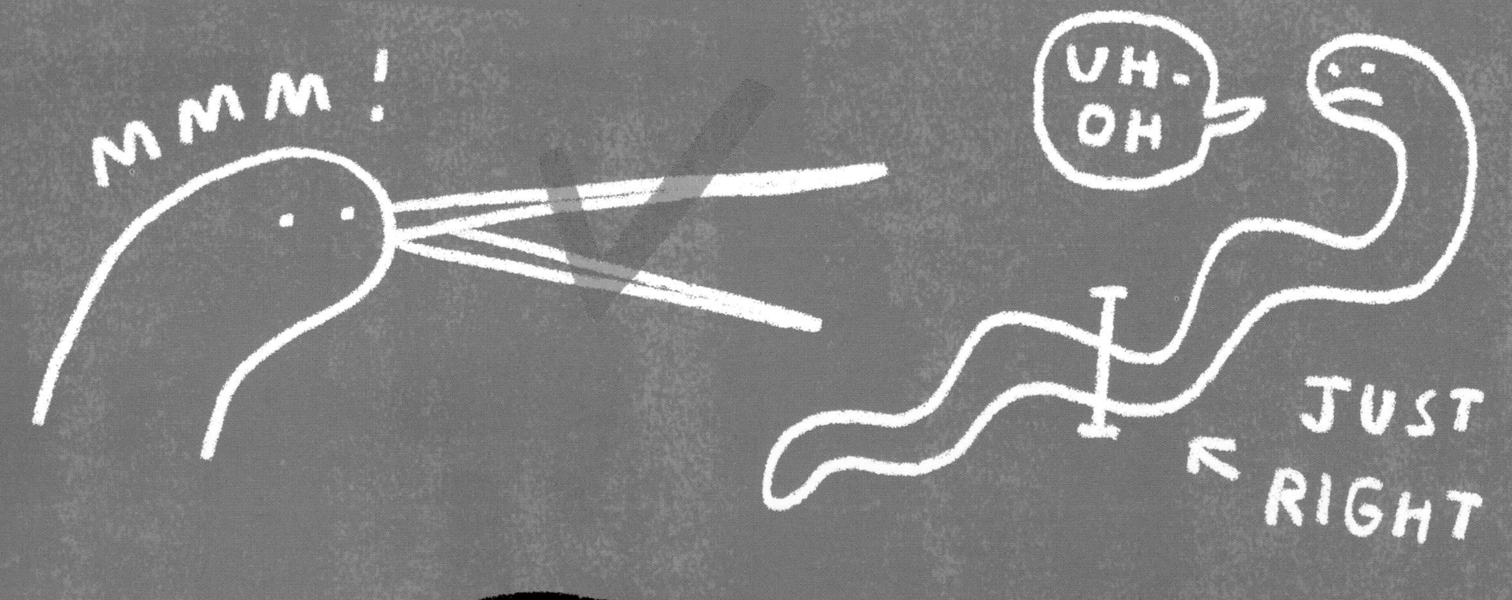

BU[illegible] BI[illegible]D CA[illegible] S[illegible]LLO[illegible] [illegible]A[illegible].

SNAKE IS **AFRAID.**

SNAKE CANNOT ESCAPE.

KNOT
CAN...

KNOT!

BIRD CANNOT SWALLOW A GREAT BIG KNOT.
SNAKE IS SAFE.
WHEW!
BIRD FLIES OFF.
NOT BAD, KNOT.
LICK!
AW!

KNOT STILL CANNOT
SLITHER.
WHEE!
HISSSSS
KNOT STILL CANNOT
HISS.
KNOT STILL CANNOT SWALLOW HIS SUPPER
WHOLE.
THAT'S OK, I'M NOT HUNGRY.

OR SHED HIS

SKIN.

OR

CLIMB

OR

SWIM

OR

BEND.

OR TASTE

DANGER.

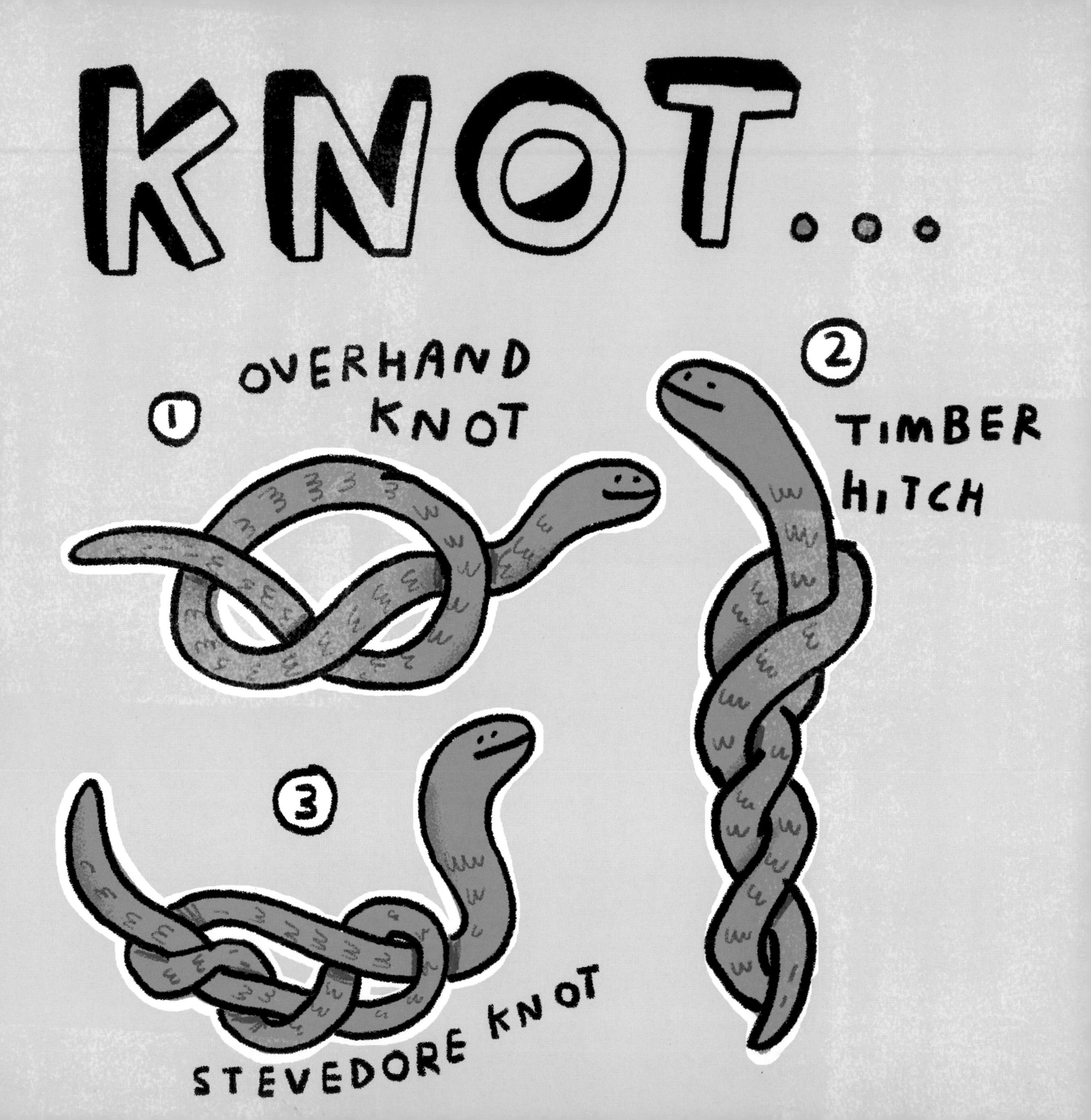
KNOT...
1 OVERHAND KNOT
2 TIMBER HITCH
3 STEVEDORE KNOT

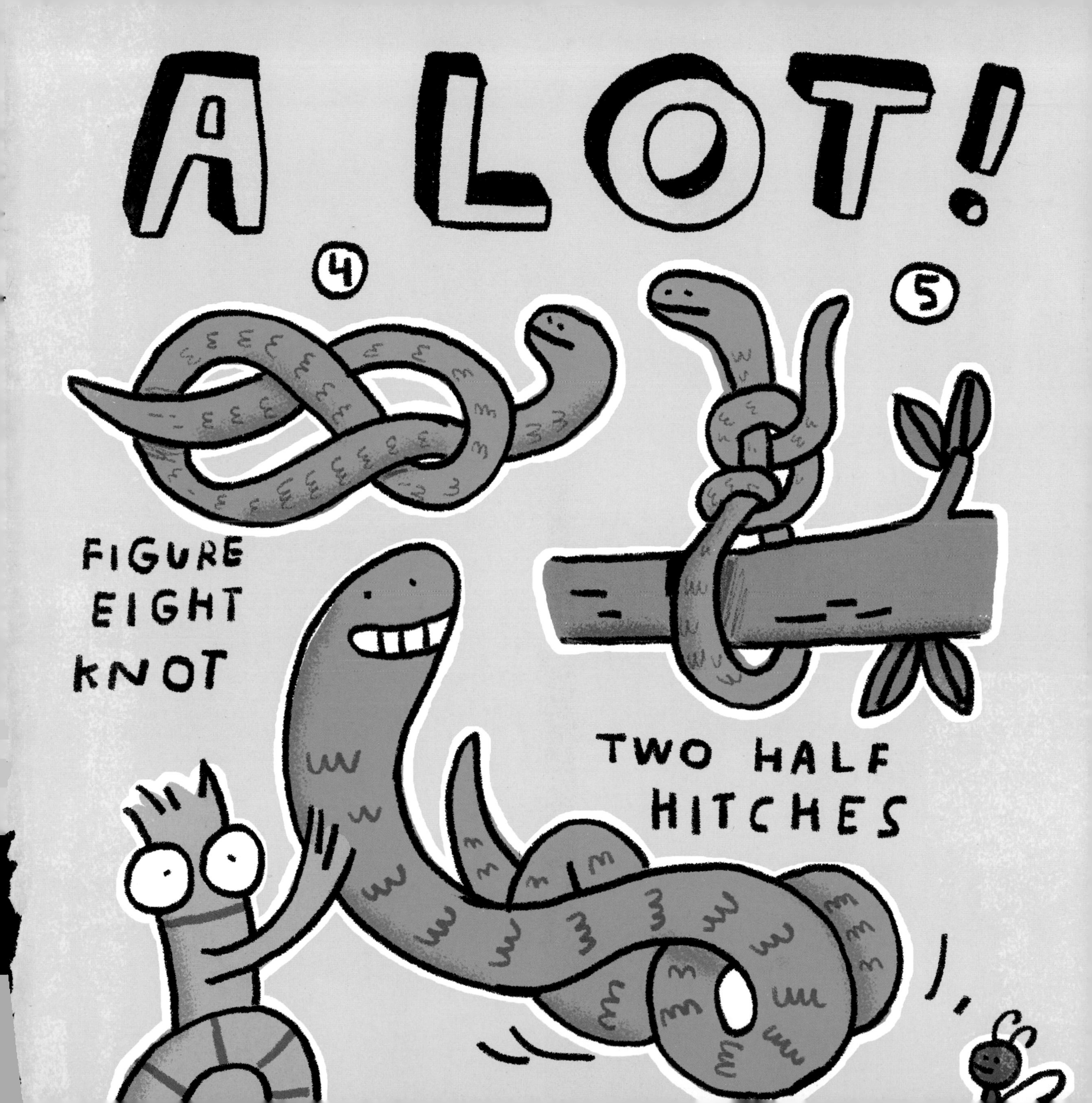
A LOT!
4
FIGURE EIGHT KNOT
5
TWO HALF HITCHES

HIGH FIVE!
BOWLINE KNOT